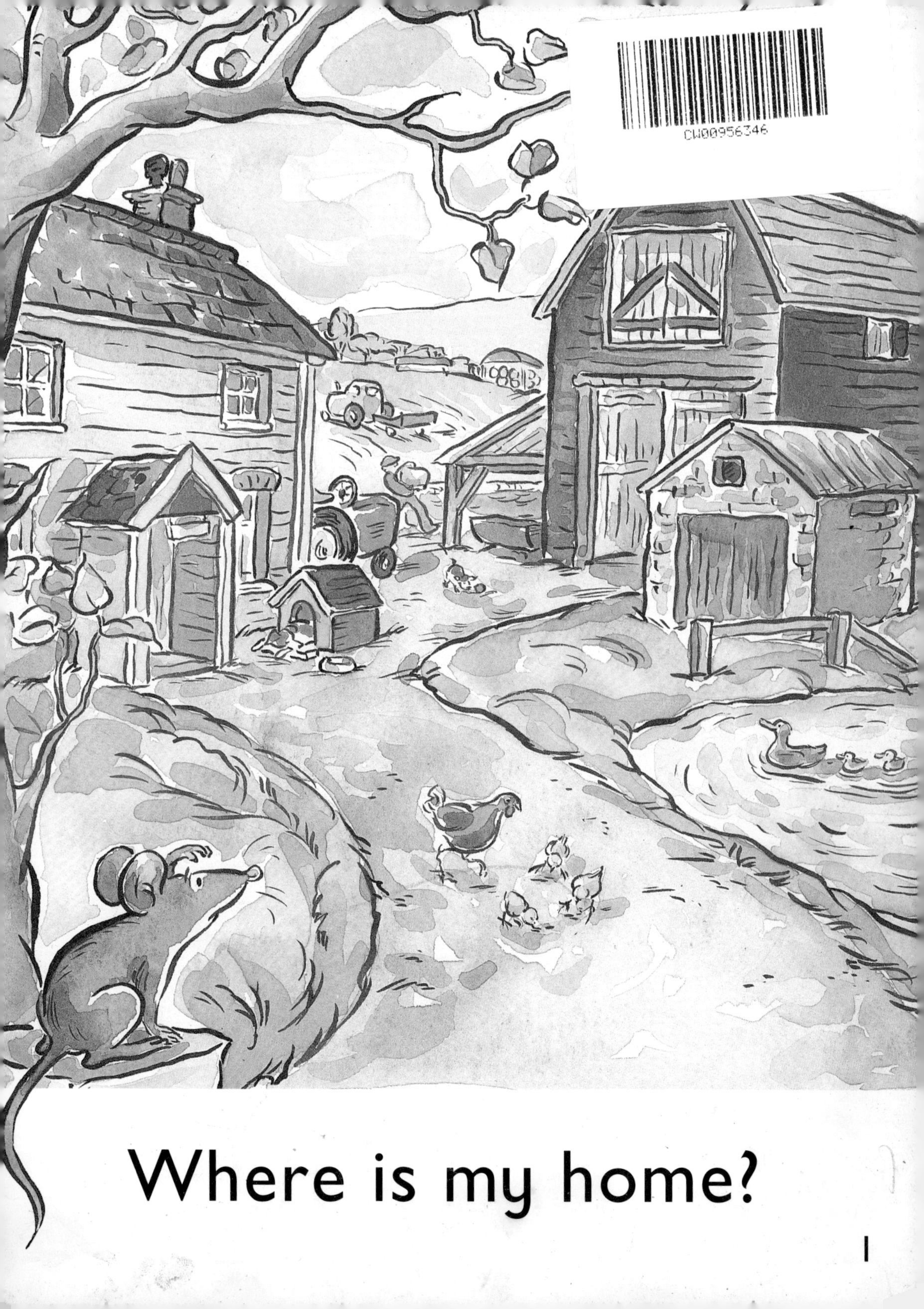

Where is my home?

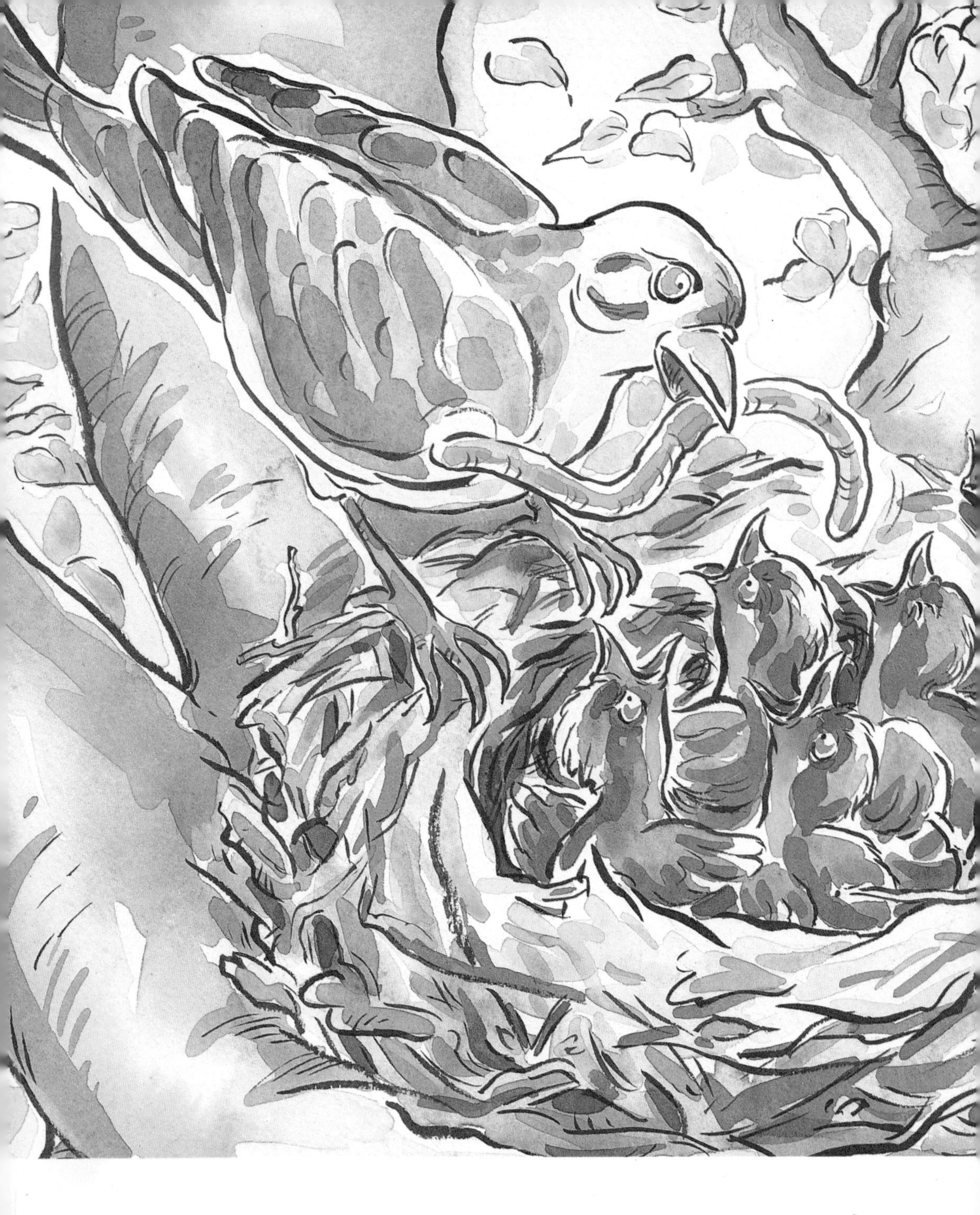

Is it in here?

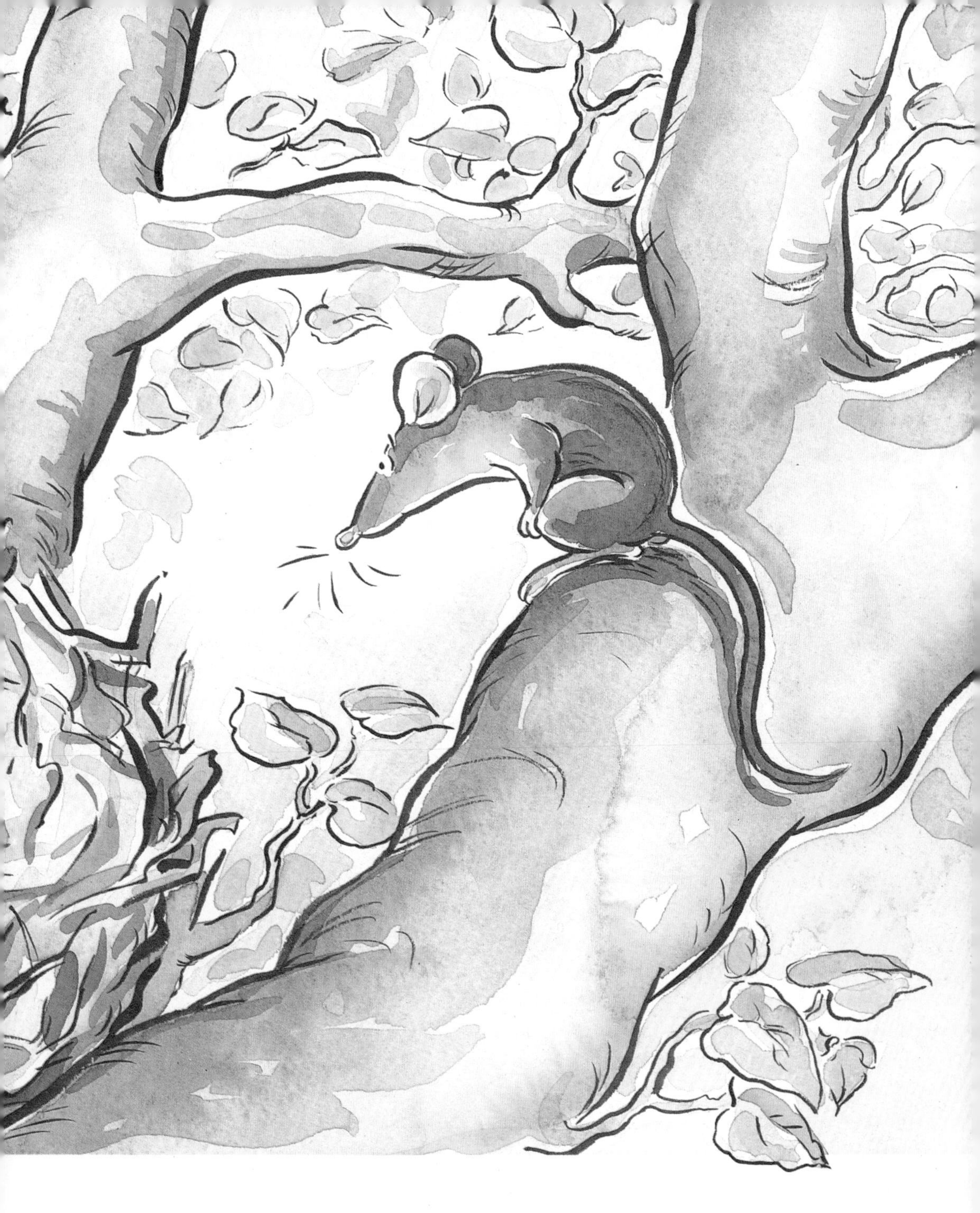

No, not in here.

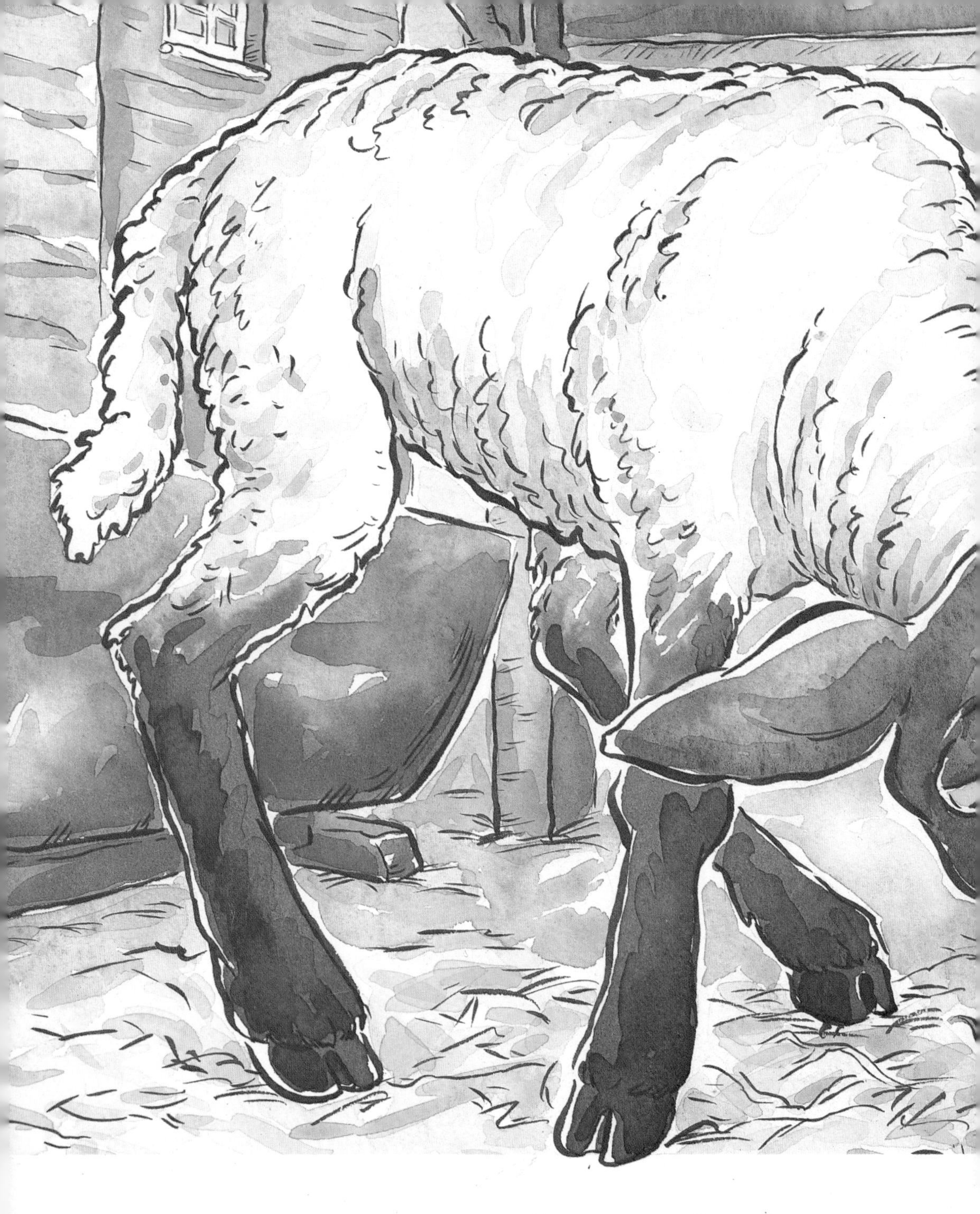

Is it in here?

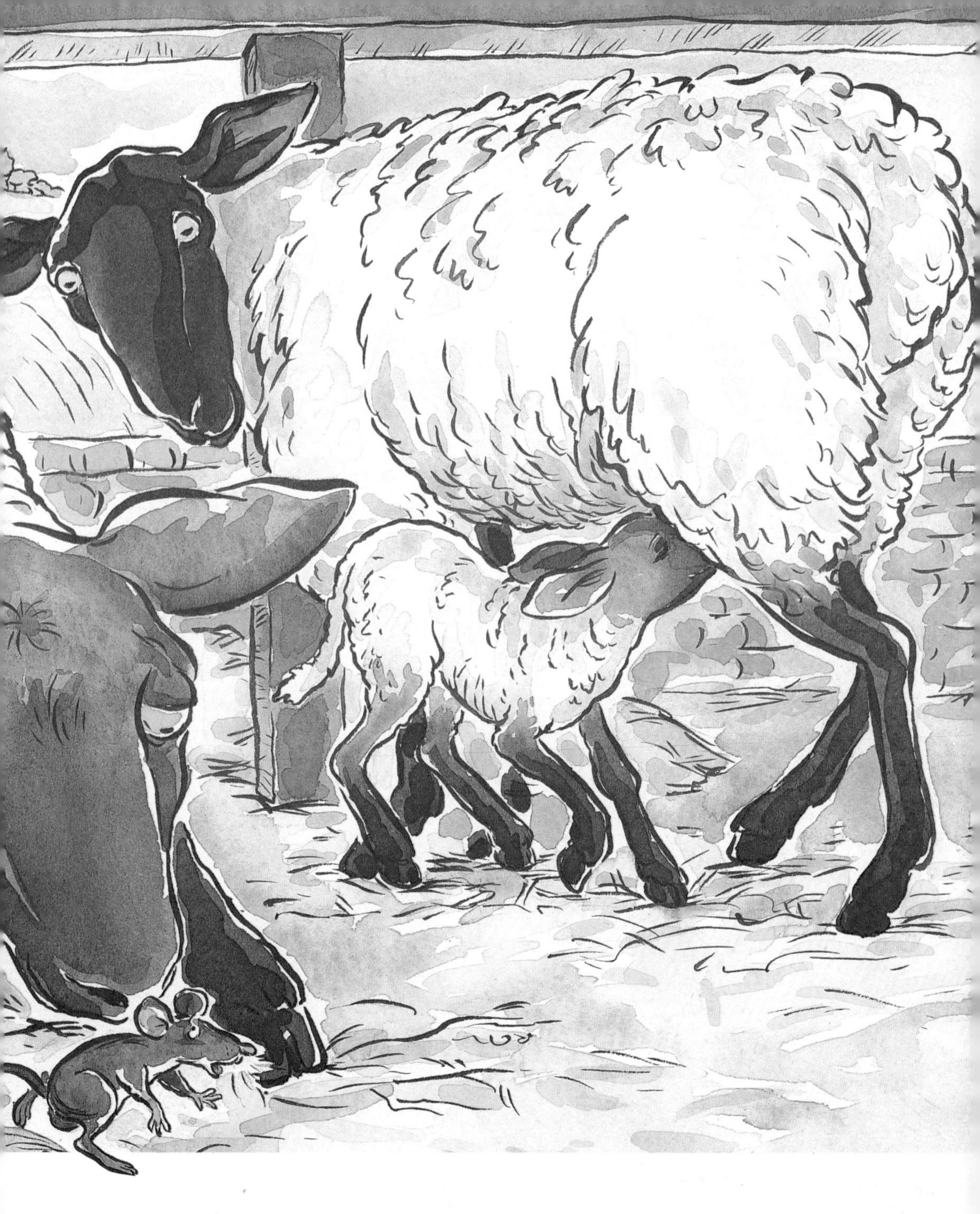

No, not in here.

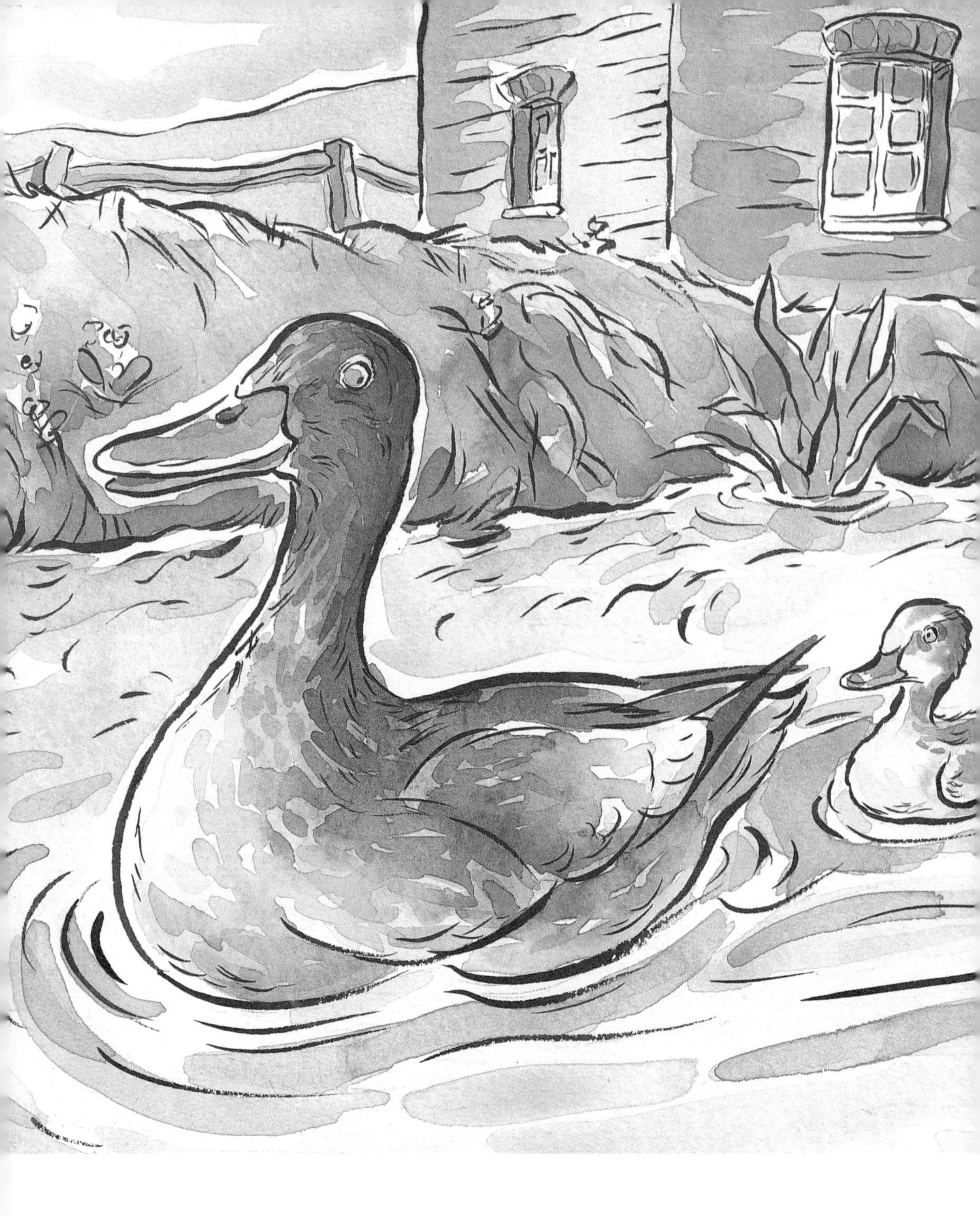

Is it in here?

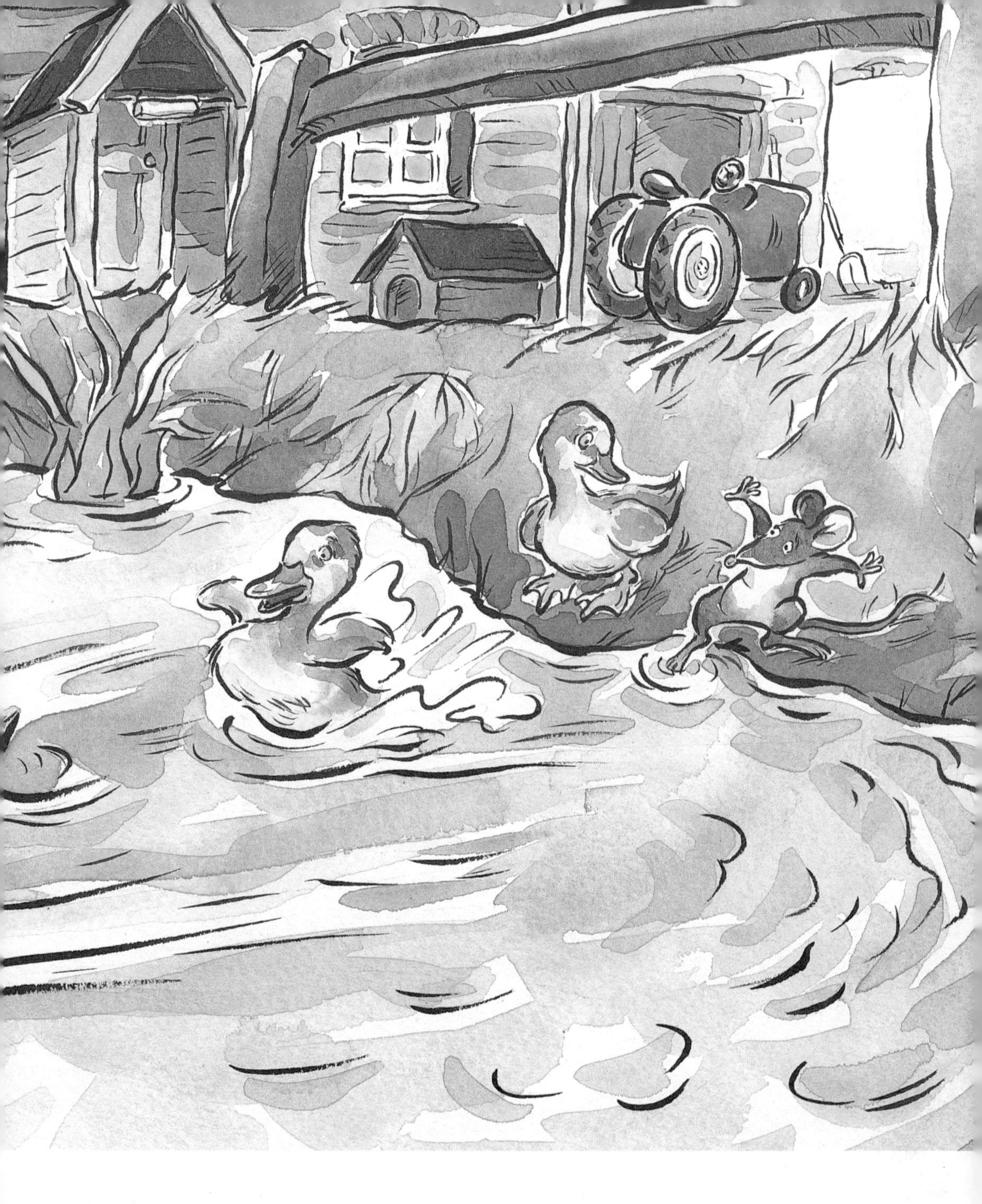

No, not in here.

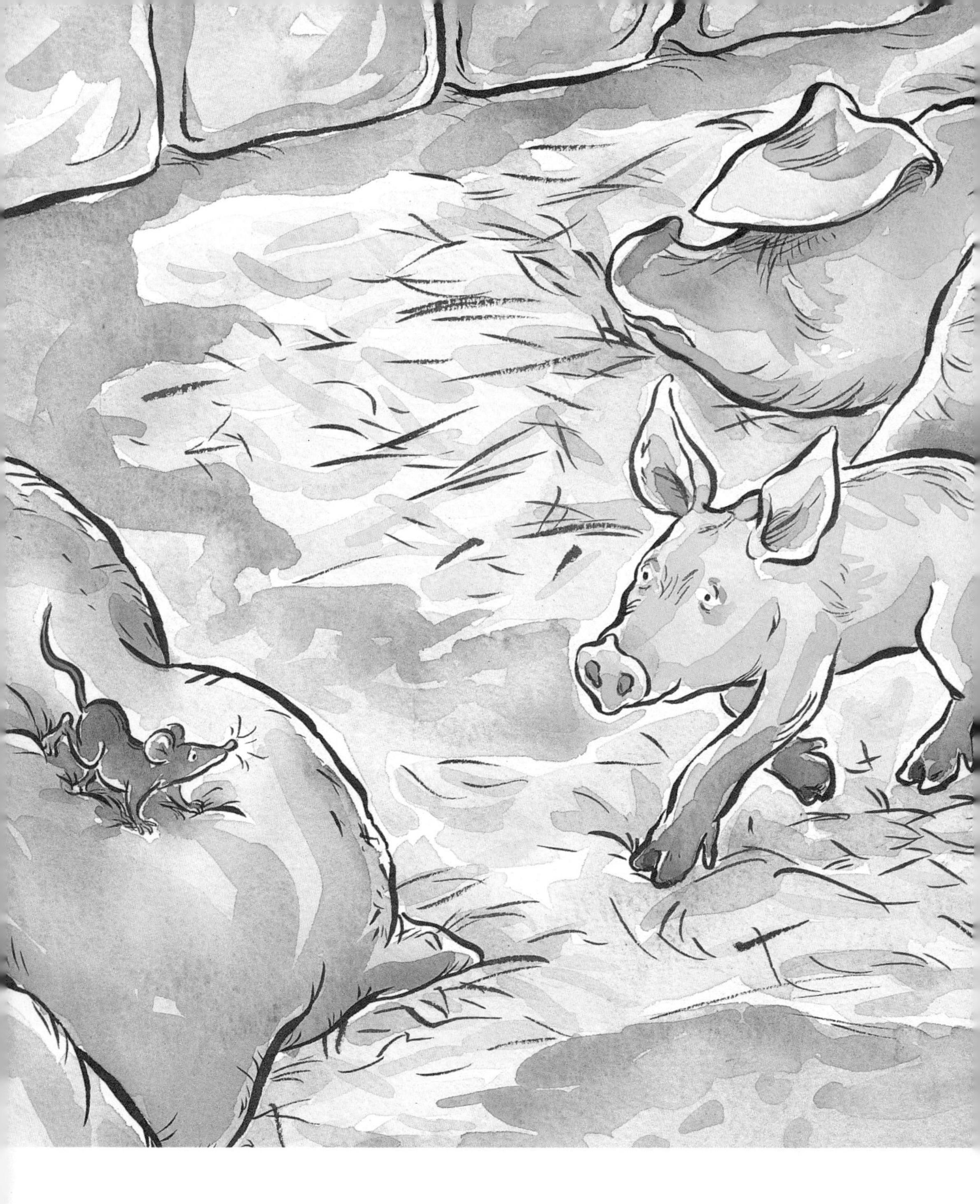

Is it in here?

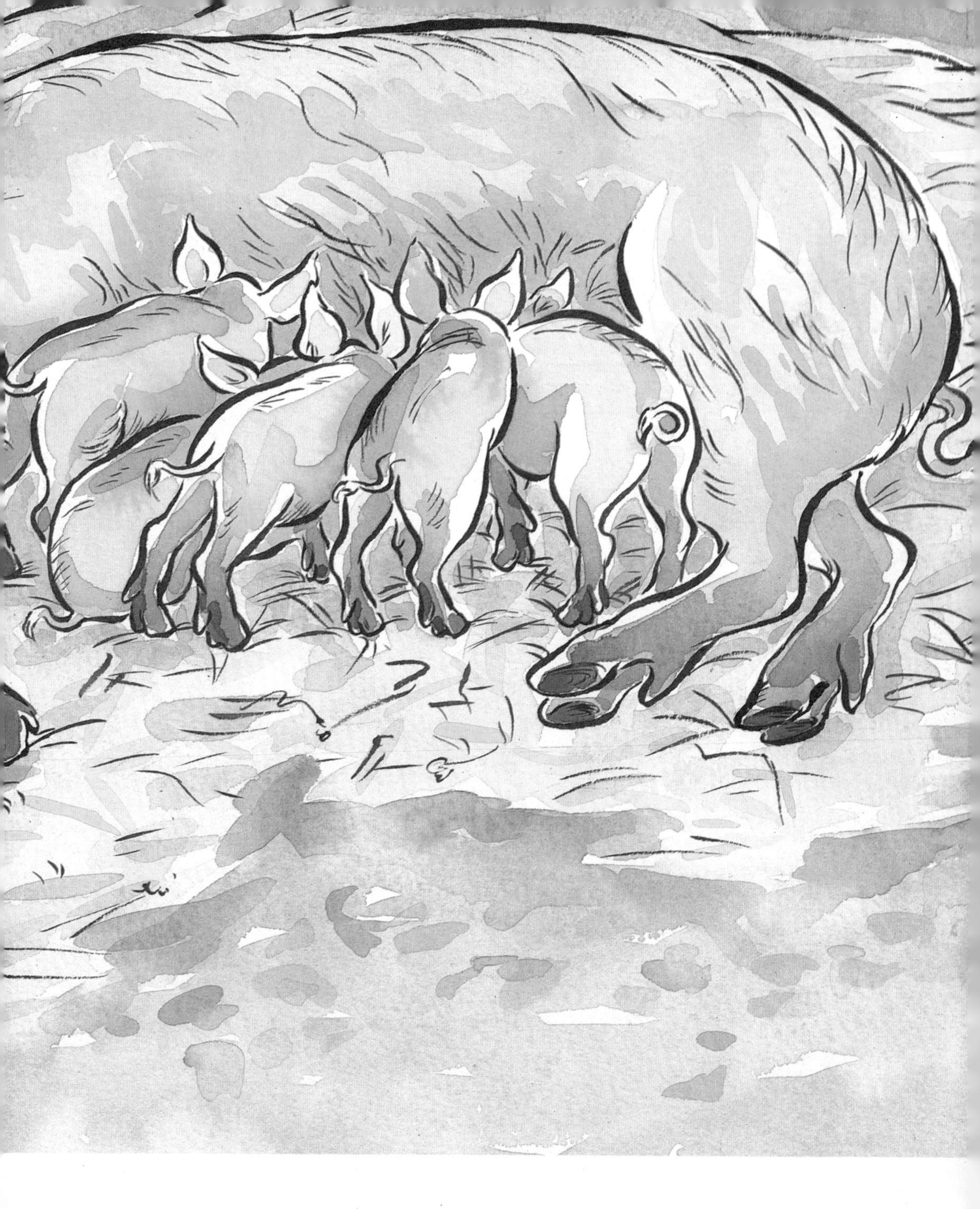

No, not in here.

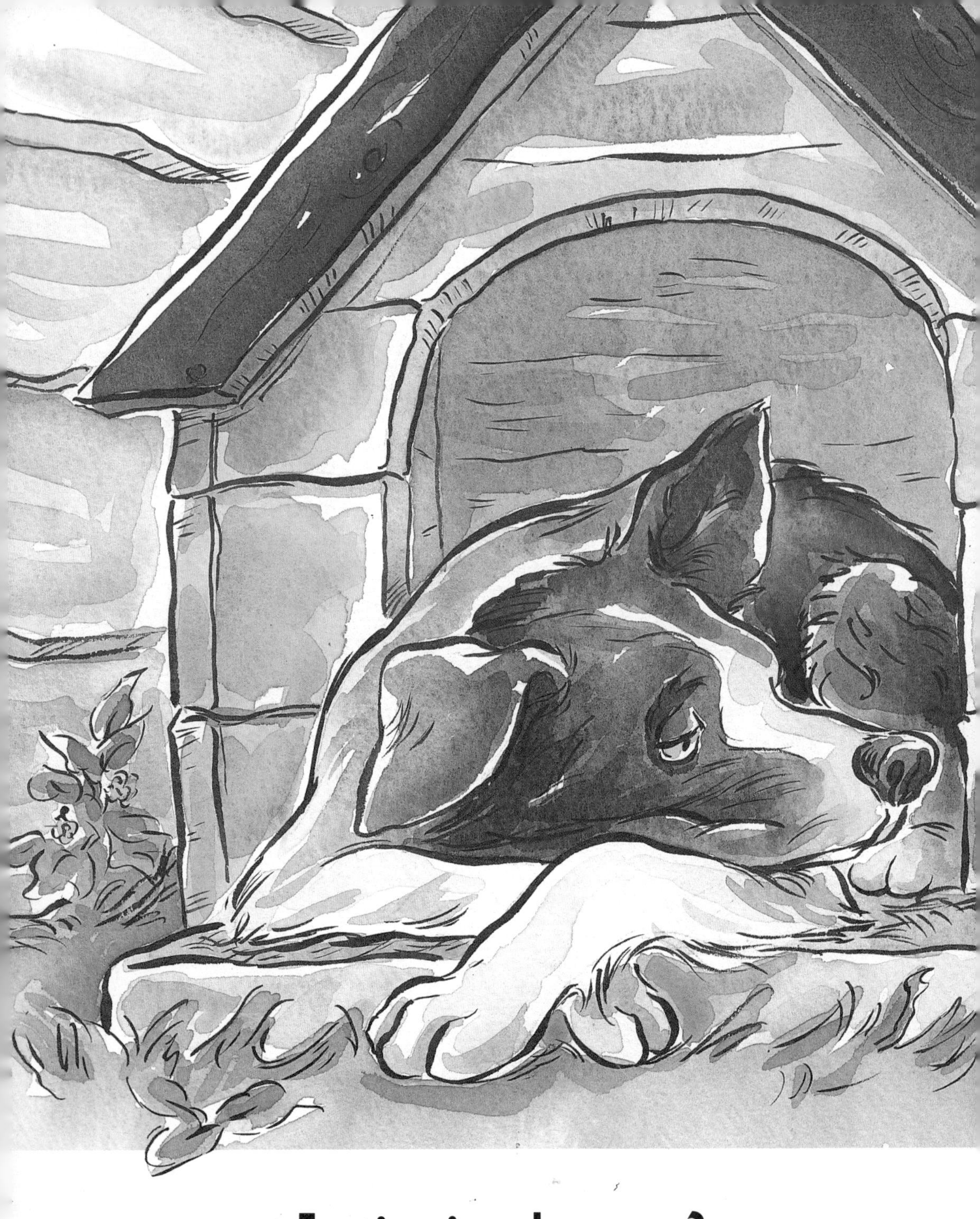

Is it in here?

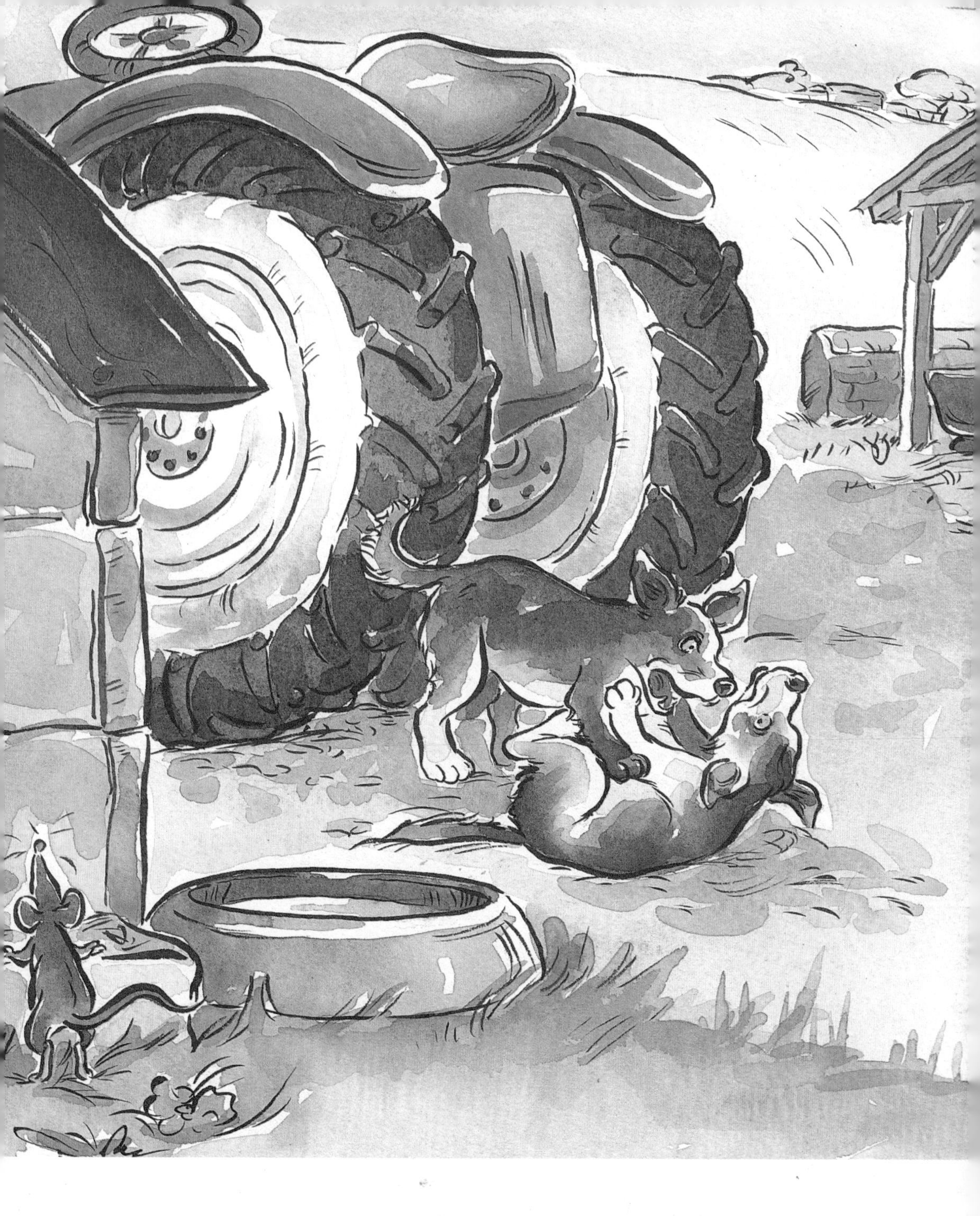

No, not in here.

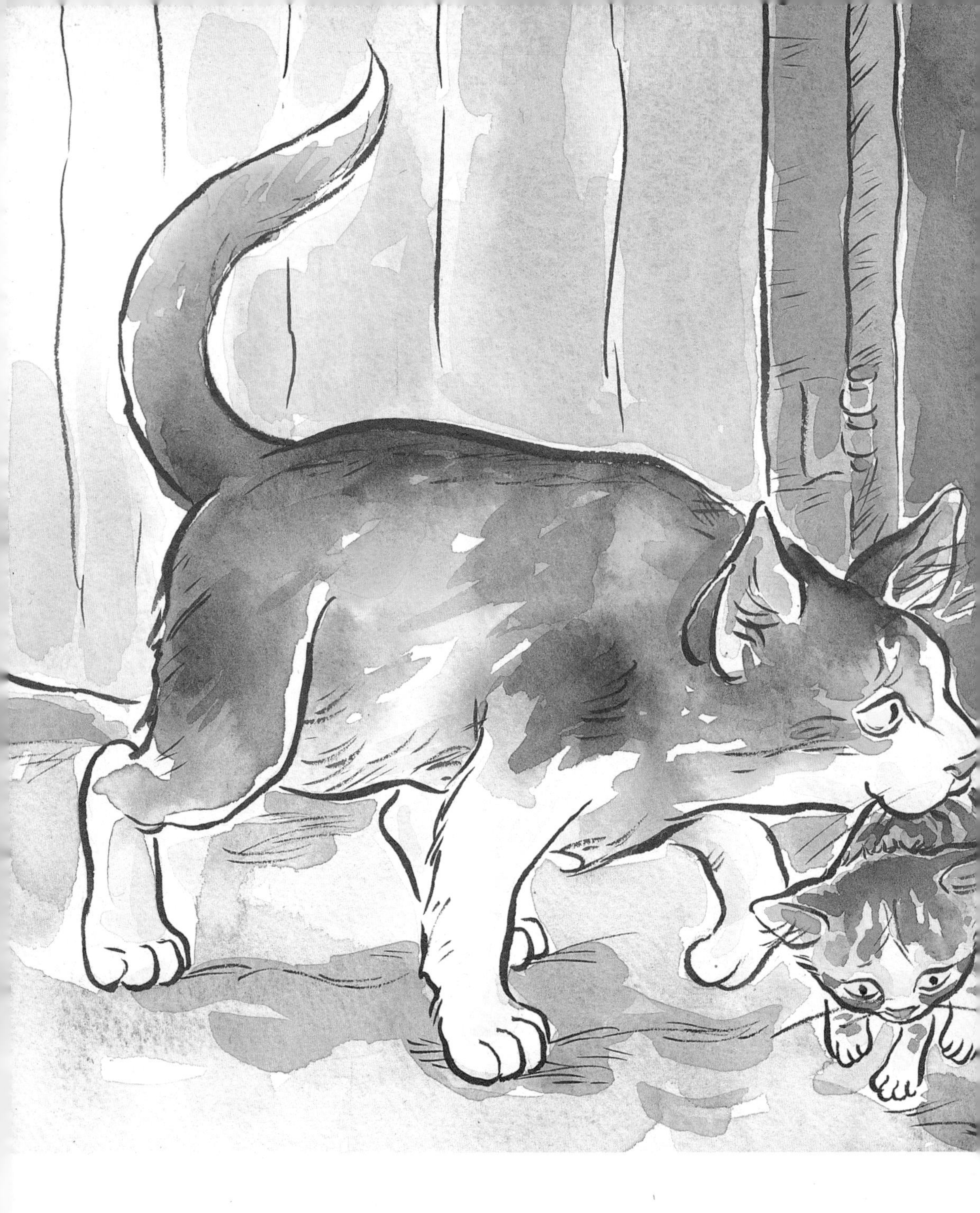

Is it in here?

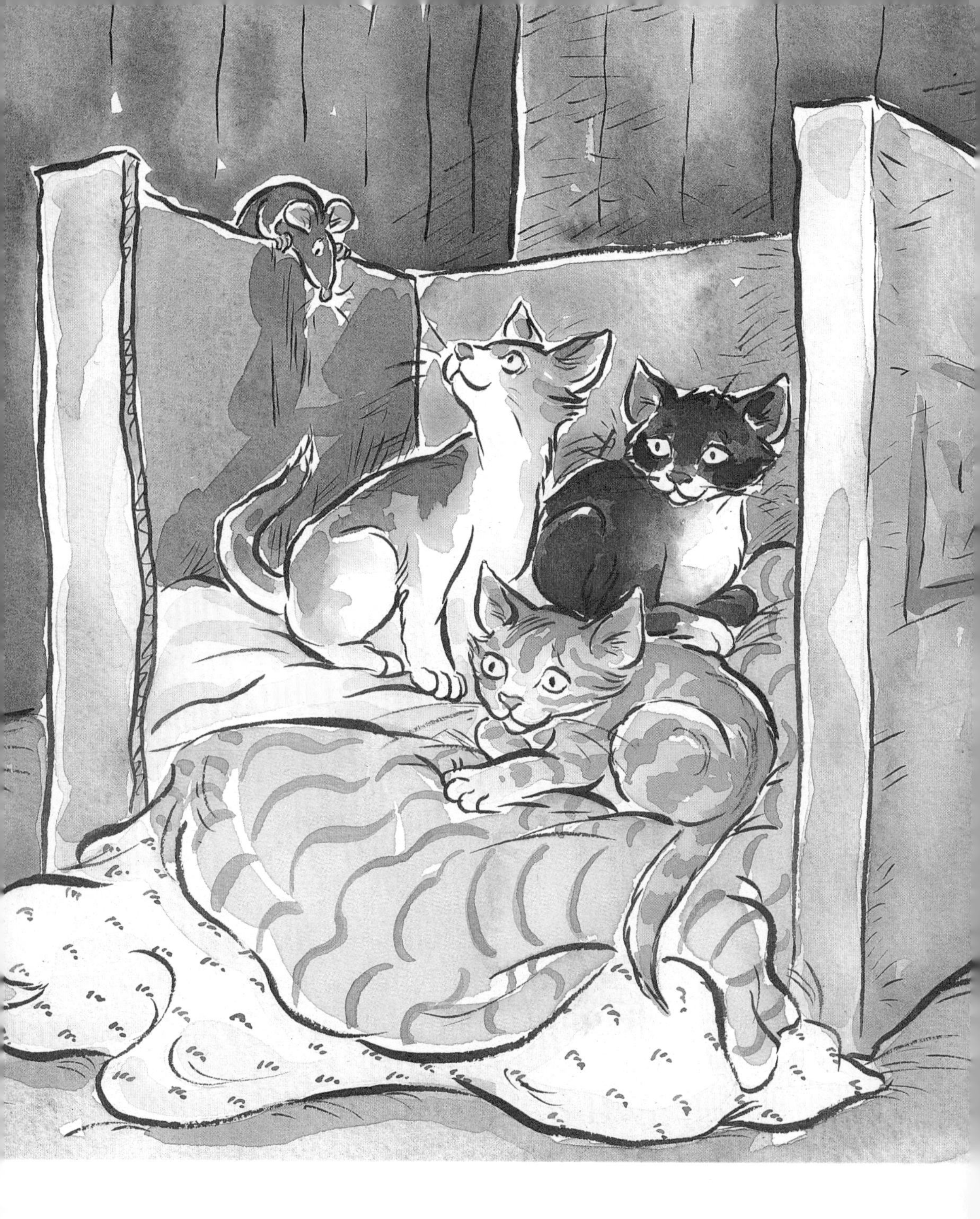

No, not in here.

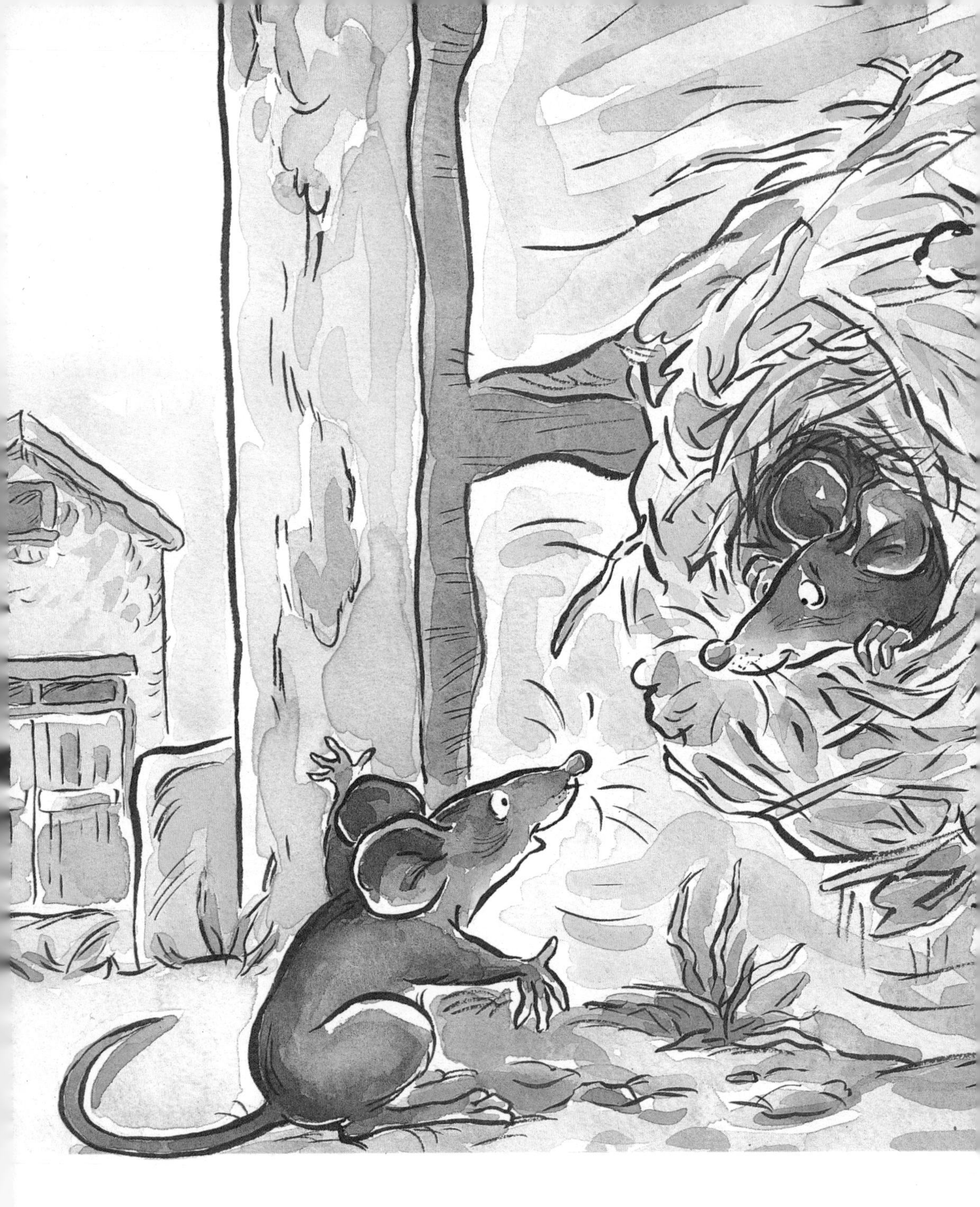

Is it in here?

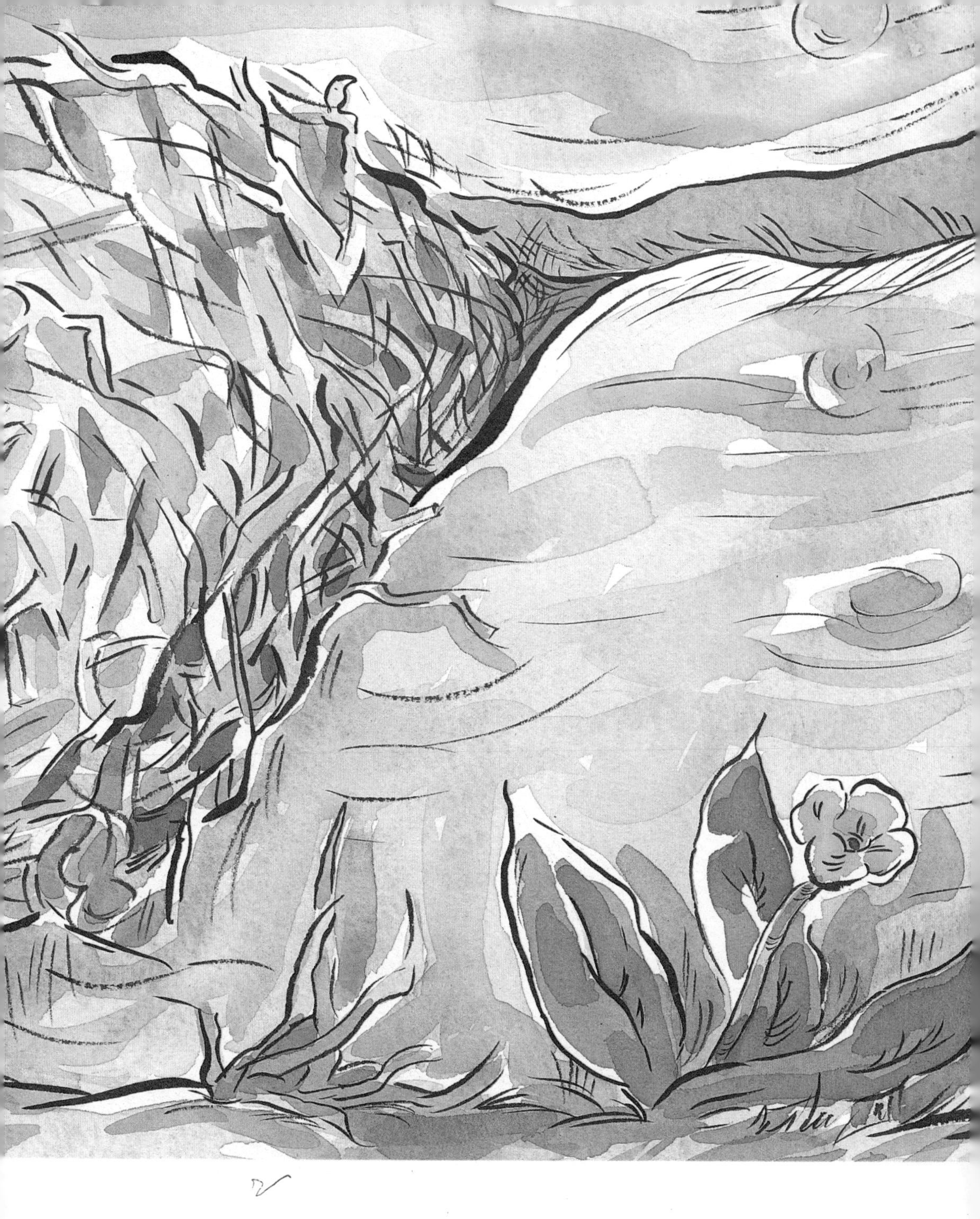

Yes. Here it is.

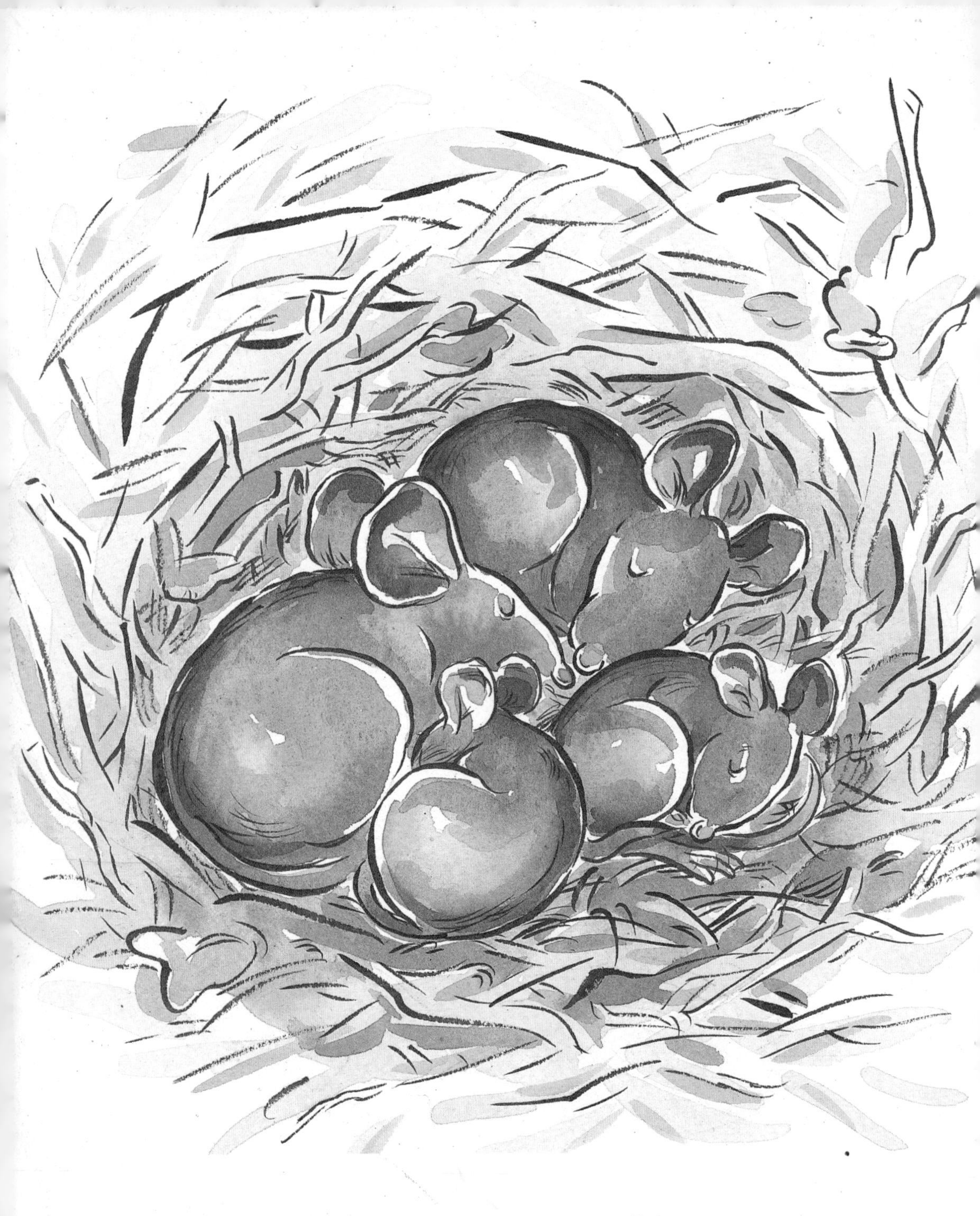

My home is here.